This book belongs to

When you finish this book, it will be all about you—what you're like and what you like to do. It will be about ways you're special, and ways you're like other people. It will be a portrait of you.

Have you ever thought about how amazing you are? Your body is a fantastic machine; it takes whatever you eat and turns your meals into YOU—your beating heart, your breathing lungs, and all the rest of you. You have a mind that can be smart in many different ways. You can learn about the past, and you can make the future. You have a spirit that can care about others.

In this book, you'll learn a lot about yourself, and you'll probably like what you learn!

If this book belongs to you, write your name in the box above and fill out the self-portrait pages as you come to them. Keep the book in a safe place, so you'll always know what you were like right now, this year.

If you're sharing the book with others, the name of your group, school, or library belongs in the box above, and you should be careful **not** to write in the book. Instead, you can copy the self-portrait pages on a copy machine. Then all of you can staple a set together, and everyone will have a book ALL ABOUT YOU to keep.

To all the kids who contributed to this book through their photographs, their stories, their drawings, and their ideas—

and to all those who will use it—

please think of this as a celebration of yourselves!

All About You

A Kids Bridge Book from
The Children's Museum, Boston

by Aylette Jenness

This book series is based on The Kids Bridge exhibit created by Joanne Jones-Rizzi and Aylette Jenness, which was designed to help children understand and appreciate cultural diversity and work against prejudice and discrimination. Exhibit team: Fabiana Chiu, Brad Larson, Dan Spock, John Spalvins, Signe Hanson, and Dorothy Merrill.

Designed and Illustrated by Kaeser & Wilson Design, Ltd.
Photographs by Max Belcher

The New Press   THE NEW PRESS   New York

All About You

Published in the United States by The New Press, New York
Distributed by W. W. Norton & Company, Inc.,
500 Fifth Avenue, New York, NY 10110

ISBN   1-56584-053-4

LC   93-83811

Designed and illustrated by Kaeser & Wilson Design, Ltd.

Photographs by Max Belcher

Established in 1990 as a major alternative to the large, commercial publishing houses, The New Press is the first full-scale nonprofit American book publisher outside of the university presses. The Press is operated editorially in the public interest, rather than for private gain; it is committed to publishing in innovative ways works of educational, cultural, and community value that, despite their intellectual merits, might not normally be "commercially" viable. The New Press's editorial offices are located at the City University of New York.

Printed in the United States of America

Production by Kim Waymer

94 95 96 97   9 8 7 6 5 4 3 2 1

ACKNOWLEDGMENTS

This book series is based on the work of The Kids Bridge exhibit development team, consultants, members of the Multicultural Program Advisory Board, and responses from the visiting public.

All About You draws on the work begun many years ago by the Children's Museum staff and board, particularly: the Ethnic Discovery Project, a pioneering curriculum development research project from the early days of multicultural studies; the Meeting Ground exhibits, the first community exhibitions, which informed all later work on collaborating with people to explore their culture and their heritage; and especially the work of Sylvia Sawin.

It would be impossible to name all the staff members who, over the years, have explored this subject through discussion, public and school programs, curricula, and exhibits, and whose ideas influenced this book.

Thanks to the following people for their many helpful suggestions on the manuscript:

Dorothy Merrill, Leslie Swartz, Lisa W. Kroeber; Joanne Jones-Rizzi and Zora Rizzi; Signe and Siri Hanson; Linda Warner and Kay Perdue.

Thanks to:
Helen McElroy, Cecilia Franzel, Susan Schroeder, their third- and fourth-grade students, and Jan Shafer and her fifth- and sixth-grade students, all from the Cambridge Friends school, for their collaboration: their criticisms, their suggestions, and their heartfelt writings.

Thanks to:
Alexa Trefonides and her students at the Agassiz Community Center After-school Program, for their beautiful silhouettes.

Thanks to Carlos and Ernesto Diaz for their drawings.

Thanks to the adults whose photographs appear in the chapter "Who Are You Like? Who's Like You?"

Thanks to Howard Gardner for his much-needed ideas on multiple intelligences.

Thanks to Dawn Davis and the staff at The New Press for their enthusiasm and hard work on this project.

The Kids Bridge exhibit was generously supported by:
Jessie B. Cox Charitable Trust
The Boston Foundation
The Boston Globe Foundation
Lotus Development Corporation
Digital Equipment Corporation
The Riley Foundation
The Xerox Foundation
Apple Computers, Incorporated, Community Affairs
The Foley, Hoag and Eliot Foundation.

CONTENTS

Glossary: definitions of some words in this book that may be new to you

1

First of All

Where in the World Are You?

Well, you're in our galaxy, the Milky Way—and you're on the planet earth. You're in the Americas—and you're probably somewhere in the United States. You live in a city or town, and you live on a particular street, in a particular building.

Kids live in all kinds of homes—small, large, shared, temporary—in the city, the suburbs, or the country. Some kids move a lot, and some have lived in the same home all their lives.

How about you— where do you live?

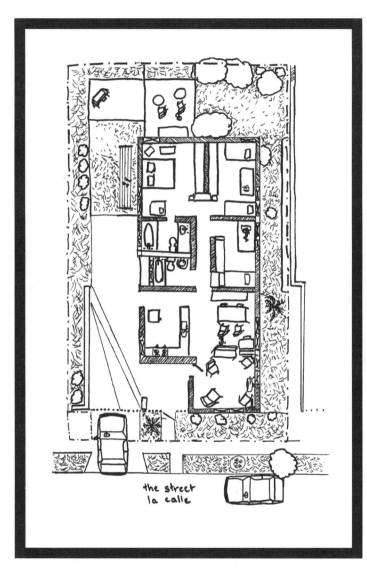

This is a floor plan of the home of the Diaz-Bello family in Puerto Rico, a Caribbean island that's part of the United States. Ernesto and Carlos Diaz made this drawing as though they were in the air, looking down on their house (without its roof!).

Here's a drawing that a girl in New England made of her home. She sketched it from across the street.

You have a space in your home where you sleep, and where you keep your clothes and special things you like.

Some kids share a room with brothers, sisters, parents, grandparents, or other members of the household. Some have a room of their own.

What about you? How would you describe your own space? big? little? lots of beds? one bed? Full of—windows? clothes? furniture? special things? messy? neat?

9

Here are some drawings kids have made of their own spaces

How do they compare with your space?

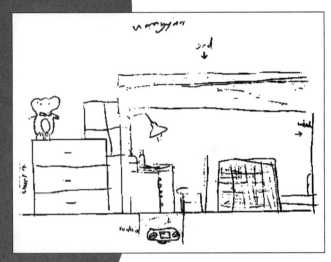

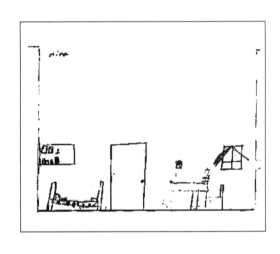

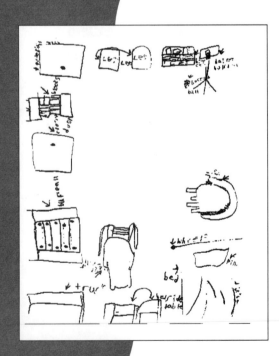

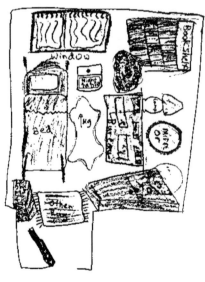

Now, are you ready to begin your own book,
All About You?

It's your turn.

HERE'S WHERE IN THE WORLD I AM

My name is

_____

and I live in this galaxy, the Milky Way—

in our world, the planet earth.

My home is in the Americas—

I live in the United States, and here's my drawing of it—

THIS IS WHERE I LIVE

I live in a part of the United States called

_____/

in the town of _____,

on a street named _____,

in a home that looks like this:

And this is a drawing of my space:

What I like about the place I live is_____

_____/

and what I don't like about it is_____

_____.

2 Who in the World Are You?

No one else in the world is **exactly** like you. At the same time, you share a lot with other kids.

Get a mirror and look carefully at yourself. Compare yourself with the kids in these pictures.

Look at each kid, and see if you can think of one way you two are alike. Can you think of a way you look different from all the other kids?

Now that you've checked yourself out, how about making a portrait of yourself? There are a lot of different ways you can do this.

You can draw a picture of yourself on the self-portrait form on page 16 (or a copy of it) or you can paste in photographs of yourself. If you're drawing, you can draw from your imagination, or you can look in a mirror while you're doing it. Remember, no one's self-portrait looks EXACTLY like them—even portraits done by great artists.

Another way to make a self-portrait is to draw a **silhouette** of yourself by using page 16 or by using a blank piece of paper. You can even do a picture of your whole body, if you have a very large piece of wrapping paper. A silhouette is an outline, and you can fill it in any way you like.

Y ou can make more than one!

If you're doing your whole body, choose a pose that says something about yourself. If you like to play softball, you could wear your hat and hold a bat. If you like to dance, start to dance and then FREEZE; hold a position that you think will look good. Do you like to read? Get a book!

On this page are some pictures kids have made of themselves. They started with their silhouettes.

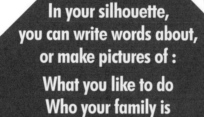
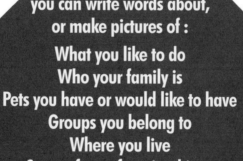

In your silhouette,
you can write words about,
or make pictures of :

What you like to do
Who your family is
Pets you have or would like to have
Groups you belong to
Where you live
Some of your favorite things
People you admire
What you daydream about

Here's how to make a silhouette. You'll need to find a partner to help you.

1. Find a lamp that will throw a strong light on a wall.

2. Tape your paper up on the wall.

3. Sit with your profile (one side of your face) almost touching the paper. Be sure your forehead, nose, mouth, and chin are on the paper, and don't worry if your paper is too small to get the back of your head on the paper. Hold very still!

4. Ask your partner to draw your outline very carefully.

5. Trade around, and draw your partner's outline.

6. Add details to your portrait.

15

A PORTRAIT OF ME

This is what I look like—

by_____.

What Kind of a Person Are You?

You're probably a person of many and varied personality traits, and you probably have skills, talents, and qualities you've never even thought about—you just took them for granted.

It's also true that, as you grow, what's important to you may change. So something you may feel bad about now, may be really unimportant later. For instance, some famous and wonderful actors were very shy when they were kids and had few friends. Some scientists got terrible grades in school.

Some people may try to put you down because of your color or religion or the language you speak—or because of things like wearing glasses, using a wheelchair, or even weighing a lot more or less than they do! This can be really painful and can make you feel terrible.

If people **discriminate** against you, if they're mean to you because you're different in some way from them, there are things you can do about it.

You can turn to your family, a teacher, or some other grown-up for help. You can ask your friends to stand by you. Sometimes you can stand up for yourself and say that your feelings are being hurt and that you don't like the way you're being treated. You may be able to say that you're proud of whatever it is that they're criticizing.

And if you want, you could join with others to help educate people about their prejudices—the way they judge people without knowing them very well. Have you ever tried any of these?

Sometimes kids think there's just one way you're **supposed to be**, and they may feel bad about themselves if they aren't like that.

But, you know, what's considered good in one school or neighborhood is very often different from what's "good" in another school or neighborhood. In one place, getting good grades in school may be a big deal. In another place, being good in sports may be considered more important.

18

Maybe the most important thing you can do is to know and like yourself. Check out the words below and decide which of them describe you. (Be honest—nobody's perfect, you know!) You could think about the words you like, and use them when you get to the forms in the next few pages.

quiet	noisy	shy	outgoing
friendly	suspicious	thoughtful	quick-witted
hard-working	clumsy	athletic	helpful
angry	kind	creative	careful
wise	relaxed	worried	careless
loving	responsible	determined	talkative
eager	weak	greedy	timid
dreamy	aggressive	outgoing	forgiving
laid-back	proud	self-respecting	trusting
daring	adventurous	tough	loyal
creative	careful	sloppy	lazy
energetic	self-confident	fearful	impatient
independent	funny	dependent	cheerful

What Kinds of Smart Are You?

Let's think about what "smart" means. In school, it usually means getting good grades. But grades only measure **some** kinds of smart in **some** kinds of subjects for **some** kinds of kids. If you have a hard time learning something, or speak a different language from English, or don't know much about the kinds of things being taught, you may not get good grades. But this doesn't mean you aren't a smart person in math or language arts or science or some other area.

Besides "school smart," there are lots of other very important ways of being intelligent.

Are you good at getting along with other people? That's a really important skill to have. If more people in the world tried to get better at that, the world would be a more peaceful place, wouldn't it?

Can you get your ideas across to other people? Can you tell a good story? You might be a fine teacher or writer or actor.

Are you good at sports? Music? Art? These are wonderful talents to have. Can you think of people you admire who are smart in these ways?

On the next pages you can write about yourself some more. You're not bragging when you write about being smart or when you consider things about yourself that you really like. Liking yourself doesn't put anyone else down, and it helps you to be happy and good at what you want to do.

Below are some things kids have written about themselves. See how many different ways there are to be?

WHAT DO YOU LIKE TO DO?

"I like to play sports, take karate, collect baseball cards, eat, tell jokes, and trade cards."

"I like to play street hockey and ride my bike."

"I like to read, hang out with my buddies, and I like to talk for hours without saying anything."

21

Here are some things kids have said about themselves.

"I'm good at soccer and karate. I'm not good at telling jokes."

"I think I'm good at swimming, writing, reading, telling how people feel, and other things. I think I'm not good at draw ing, diving, jogging, and many other things."

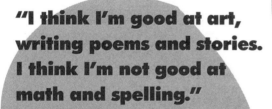

"I think I'm good at sharing, forgiving, and comebacks. I'm not good at helping around the house."

"I think I'm good at art, writing poems and stories. I think I'm not good at math and spelling."

"I think I am good at school work and athletic activites. I am not very good at keeping quiet and holding in all my ideas. Sometimes I blurt things out at the wrong times."

"Here are some ways I'm smart: I think I'm good at mysteries, sports, and reading. I think I'm not good at keeping my temper and reading out loud."

"I think I'm good at swimming and ice skating."

"Here are some things I'm good at: drawing, painting, reading, and spelling. I don't think I'm good at most sports."

"I'm good at reading, writing, and making friends. I'm not good at spelling."

ALL (well, some, anyway) ABOUT ME

My name is_____

and I've been on the planet earth for _____ years so far.

If I were to choose a bunch of words to describe myself, I'd say I'm a_____

_____kind of kid.

Not to brag, but I think I'm pretty good at _____

_____

and _____.

I think I'm not so good at_____(yuck!).

One thing I want to get better at is_____

because _____.

When I can do whatever I want to do, I like to _____

_____.

And that's all I have to say right now!

23

(Some) MORE ABOUT ME

Thinking about myself, I'd say I'm more

☐ funny   ☐ cautious   ☐ competitive

☐ serious   ☐ daring   ☐ cooperative

My family thinks I should _____

_____,

and I think I should _____

_____.

Something I really like about myself is_____

_____

_____.

When I grow up, one of the things I might like to do is _____

_____

because _____.

Right now, if I could do one thing to change the world, I'd

_____.

THINGS I LIKE (A lot!)

My favorite colors right now are _____

_____,

and what I really like to wear is _____

_____.

My favorite foods are _____

_____.

Somebody who I think is great is _____.

A hobby of mine is _____

_____.

My favorite TV shows are _____

_____.

Music groups I like are _____

_____.

The movie and TV stars I like best right now are _____

_____.

My favorite sport to **watch** is _____,

and my favorite sport to **play** is _____.

3 The Story of Your Life

As soon as you're born, you start being part of the world, and you start having a history. Thinking about your history can be fun, exciting, painful, and interesting—all at once. Things you remember tell you a lot about yourself; what makes you happy, what hurts you, what's important to you.

Here are some things kids have said about their own lives. When you use the next form, you can write your own history. It's yours to keep to yourself or to share with others if you want.

"I hardly know anything about my birth. There was a lightning storm. Dad got lost driving to the hospital. Then I was born. I don't know how to describe myself exactly; I like to spin around in a chair, I like to play in my room, I like to use computers. I like to build houses for myself out of pillows. I **dislike** the smell of gasoline, being sick, getting bored, getting in fights with my sister, war, pollution!"

"I weighed 6 pounds, 10 ounces when I was born. My first words were 'Big Bird' and 'mommy.' I am black. My eyes are brown, and my hair is dark brown. I am growing up to be independent and I am growing up slowly and to be me."

"I'm really scared of weird noises in the dark."

"I was born in El Salvador. I never cried when I was little. I ate a lot when I was little. I was allergic to milk a lot when I was little in El Salvador. My first time on a plane was coming to the U.S.A. from El Salvador, I was eight months old. The first word I said was 'Mama.' My goals are to graduate, catch a shark, scuba dive, and finish an adult book."

"The worst thing that ever happened to me is that my aunt died in a car accident. The best thing that happened is I got to be a big sister."

"One of the best things that ever happened to me is getting a guinea pig. The worst thing that ever happened to me is homework."

27

"I don't like vegetables, language, cake, gymnastics, reading, writing, and going to the dentist. I love ice cream, board games, TV, Leggo, candy, drawing, and math."

"The worst thing that ever happened to me is that I almost drowned, I nearly got killed by a car, and my sister was born. The best thing that ever happened is that I got a younger brother who is older than my sister and he is my good brother."

"Most of my family lives in Honduras. It is very hard for me sometimes because some of my uncles died before I even knew them."

"I'm really scared of falling on my face in gymnastics."

"I like when my father teases me because I get to tease him back. I don't like when I get punished."

"When I was born I weighed 4 pounds and 0 ounces. I was born in April on the 11th. As a young baby I liked to get in my mom's garbage can. I did not care if it was full or empty. Things that I dislike are mustard, relish, coleslaw, celery, peppers, bees, dissecting animals, having people die including myself, and getting lost. Here are things that are more cheerful that I like: snow, noodles, the smell of rain, taking care of people, soccer, swimming, and school."

My Life Story

I was born on _____ in the city of _____ .

I can remember something that happened when I was very young (only

_____ years old), and this is what it was:

_____

That was pretty _____to me! When I was little I

liked to_____

and I didn't like to_____at all.

I used to be really scared of _____,

and even now, sometimes I'm scared of _____.

Some important events in my life are: _____

_____

_____.

A bad thing that once happened to me is _____

_____,

but I survived!

And these are some of the things in my life so far!

4 Where Did You Come From?

We're not talking about how you were born, and we're not talking about your hometown. This is about—

Your Family

You may belong to your family by birth, adoption, or invitation. That means that you may be in a foster family that wants to take care of you because your birth family can't right now. You may be adopted, and this family will be yours for life. Some adopted kids know their birth parents, and so they may feel these are family, too. You may be born into your family, and you may live with both parents or either one of them. Maybe you live with stepparents and stepbrothers and sisters. Maybe you live with grandparents, older brothers or sisters, aunts, uncles, or cousins.

Do you have pets? Do you think of them as part of your family?

You may have informally "adopted" someone into your family—a babysitter you had for a long time, or a neighbor, or a grown-up friend of your parents who's a special friend of yours.

And over the course of your life, you'll probably be part of different kinds of families, because families grow and change, just like people do.

Family members may all be of the same race, or of different races. That means that some people in the family might be Asian, while others are white. Some might be African-American, and others Native American.

In some families, people come from different cultural backgrounds. That means they might celebrate different holidays, have special foods which are different—even speak different languages. That's what a cultural group is—people who share a common way of life. For instance, one part of the family might be Latino and another Irish-American.

If you're in families like these, you might call yourself **bi**cultural (bi- means "two") or **multi**cultural (multi- means "many"), or bi- or multiracial.

Being part of a multiracial or multicultural family can be wonderful and it can be hard. It may be hard to figure out just who you are and where you fit in. Another problem is that some people just don't understand how varied families are; they might say to an adopted kid who's of a different race from his or her parent, "How can **she** be your mom? You don't look like each other." If you're part of a "multi-" family, you'll probably have to educate people sometimes, and that can be a challenge for you.

The important thing to remember about families is that they all have the same purpose. All family members, if they possibly can, want to take care of each other, help each other, and have fun together.

On the next page is a sheet that you can use, or copy, to draw a picture of your family or put in some photographs. And there's a space for you to write something about them, too. When you're doing this, you might think about family members who live with you, and those you only see from time to time. Can you think of things all of these family members do for you, things you do for them, and things you like to do together?

"I consider my family anyone who I am close to; grandparents, parents, aunts, uncles, and cousins. Some people think that only your relatives should be considered family, but I don't. Several of my friends and parents' friends I consider family and hope they feel the same about me."

"I consider Muggsy my cat part of my family. Other people in my family are two grandpas and two grandmas, two uncles and two aunts, and two cousins."

"My biggest hopes of all are that my two grandmothers, who are very sick, will live for a very, very, long time."

"I lived in Korea almost two years and then I was adopted and came to America. One of my events is coming from Korea to America. Another event is when my sister came from Korea to America. The last event is the first day I went to school."

written about their families:

"I live with my mom in a building and in a house with my dad and stepmother. I have two cats and a bird. I used to have fish, but my cats went fishing overnight on my dresser."

"My family is a very important part of my life. My friends are a very important part of my life. The decisions I make are an important part of my life. I like cats and brown dogs."

"Some important things to my family are me, that most of us are in good health, we have homes, enough money for food and clothes, and good educations. Also for little extras like books, a television, and a radio."

My Family

Here's who's in my family

My family is_____,

and when we're together, we like to _____

_____.

Some things my family does for me are _____

_____

_____,

and some things I do for them are_____

_____.

Here are some things that are important to my family (I know because they told me!):

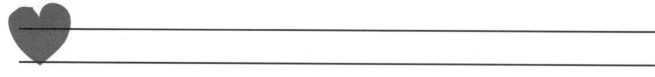

_____

_____.

Your Family History

Unless you're a Native American, your ancestors (the family members born long before you) came or were brought to the United States sometime in the last few hundred years. If you **are** a Native American, your ancestors were here long before that.

We're a country of many immigrants. We came here from Europe, Africa, Asia, the other Americas, the Caribbean— almost any place you can think of. In fact, it would probably be hard to find a country on the globe from which no one has ever come to the United States. People started coming here more than five hundred years ago, and they've been coming ever since .

Researching Your Family History

Where did your family come from? Try doing some research on your family history. You'll surely hear surprising stories, if you're a good questioner and a good listener. You may find that (like many of us here in the United States) your family members came from many different places at many different times. And for a lot of different reasons!

On the next page are some questions it might be fun to ask members of your family—the older the better! If you aren't related by birth to your family, their history is still very much your history, because it influences your life. If you live with a foster family now, you have some choices. If you see some of your relatives, you could talk to them about this. And if you don't, you could write about your foster family history because you're a part of that family now.

Here are some tips for doing family interviews with relatives:

1. Start by explaining what you're up to—that you want to learn more about your family history. Show them the form, and be sure you have their permission before you start.

2. Choose a quiet place and enough time to do it.

3. You won't be able to write down everything! Ask them to wait while you're writing—and then sit back and enjoy listening to everything **else** they have to say. These questions are just a start on learning about your family's past.

4. You can skip over questions that don't interest them and add ideas they or you **are** interested in. This is not a test!

An Interview with

_____ ,

A Member of My Family

Where were you born, and what's the earliest thing you can remember?
_____ .

What was your home like when you were little?
_____
_____ .

Did you ever move to a new home? Why did your family move?
_____ .

What did you do for fun when you were a kid? _____
_____ .

What games did you play? _____
_____ .

What was your favorite food when you were a kid?
_____ .

What kinds of clothes did you wear to school? What did you wear at
special times? _____ .

What were the rules at home when you were a kid? _____
_____ .

What did you do to help out around the house? _____
_____ .

What was elementary school like for you?
_____ .

Can you tell a funny story about our family?
_____ .

Family Travels

On page 40, you'll find a sheet entitled MY FAMILY'S TRAVELS. If you're sharing this book, copy the form. Collect some crayons, magic markers, or colored pencils.

On the world map, make a colored dot where you were born. Then choose another color and make dots where your parents or the family members you live with were born. Draw a line from each of those dots to your dot. Then choose **another** color and make dots for where the grandparents in your family were born, if you can find that out. Draw a line connecting those two generations — grandparents and parents. Can you go back one more generation? That would be the generation of your great-grandparents. If you know that some of your ancestors way back came from another country, put dots there and connect them to the last generation you know in your family.

Now look at the pattern you've made. The lines you've drawn connect you, through your family, to places you may never have been, but which have probably influenced what you're like.

If you know that some of your ancestors came from another country, but you don't know much about that region of the world, you could do some research to find out what it's like there. It's kind of interesting to think that you're linked in this way with other parts of the world.

In the United States, we have many patterns of immigration and of moving around.

■ Some families have lived in the same area for many generations.

■ Some families came here recently from another country.

■ Some families have ancestors who lived in many different places all over the world.

Which of these patterns is most like your family? Or would you describe your family history differently?

In these last pages, you've been looking at one group you belong to: your family. You also belong to larger groups, and one of these is called your cultural group. What's that? You'll find out in the next chapter.

MY FAMILY'S TRAVELS

Some of my family came from _____

_____.

And this is how they got here:_____

_____

_____.

The reason they came is _____

_____

_____.

5 What's Your Culture?
(Everybody Has at Least One)

We talked about culture earlier, remember? Your culture is the way of doing things and the way of looking at the world that you share with others. It's made up of things like your beliefs, religion, language, art, stories, and what you wear and eat.

Here are some stories kids in the United States have written about their cultures:

"My racial and cultural background is Dutch, English, Scottish, Polish, Celtic, and German. I speak English. My religious background is Christian and Jewish. We celebrate Christmas and other holidays, but not in a religious way. We eat all different kinds of food. I'm proud that I have all backgrounds."

"My mother is white with green eyes. Father is Arab and has brown eyes. I only speak English and a few words in French and Arabic. My mother speaks English and French and my father does too, plus he speaks Arabic. My mother is Christian and my Dad is Moslem. I like to have big feasts with my family and friends."

"On my mom's side we don't know very much. We don't talk about our race a lot. We are Americans."

"To describe ourselves racially: we are mostly white European with a little Spanish/South American. We are mostly American in culture. This is a country of free speech, free press; I am proud of those things."

"My racial and cultural background is European-American and Asian-American and Mexican. I speak English. We celebrate Christmas and Easter. A favorite food of my group is tacos."

"On my father's side they were all born in the United States. My mother's side was born in Barbados. Our ancestors came from Africa. Sugarcane reminds me of my family history. My family is proud of the leaders of our culture."

"My family is American! My sister and I are Indian. My Mom and Dad adopted us. My mom and dad are white-skinned. I'm proud that the Indian culture is so old, and that it has stayed the same for many years. Daddy's ancestors came from Scotland. His grandfather came on a boat because his mother died and he was tired of being in a place where everyone was poor. Mommy's ancestors came from England, but her family has lived in America for a long, long, long, time. On Easter a lot of friends always come to our house. We have an Easter egg hunt and a potluck dinner and we play games and have a big retreat and we sing and sometimes we dance!"

"My racial and cultural background is African, African-American, and Haitian. My religious background is Catholic, and my family believes in God. A favorite food for us is rice and beans."

You can see from all these stories that we have a lot of diversity across the United States. For some kids, race is very important: "I'm an African-American." "I'm Asian-American." Other kids think more about their particular group: "My family came from Vietnam eight years ago." "My grandparents are Italian and they cook Italian food." And some kids don't pay much attention to any of these things, particularly if their family has been in the United States for many generations and they live in a community where everyone is similar in culture. "I'm an American, that's all." This doesn't mean that they don't have a culture—everyone does—but that they haven't thought about it much.

No matter how you look at it, your culture is an important part of you.

For instance, think about your language. You can express your wants, your ideas, your feelings—and anyone else speaking your language will understand you.

Think about your holidays; they're probably a special time when your family gets together and celebrates in a way that's traditional and familiar to you.

Think about your food! You have favorite foods, and some of them are probably dishes passed down in your family—maybe you even help cook them yourself.

Most people are proud of their way of doing things—and it's familiar and comfortable. Unfortunately, people often feel that **their** way of doing things is better than other people's culture. This can happen between kids who go to the same school, between groups who live in the same town, and between countries.

For instance, you probably think "your" food is great, and maybe you think food you're not familiar with is WEIRD. The funny thing is that other people may feel exactly the same way about **your** food! So who's right?

The point is that we're often suspicious about things that are different, until we've gotten familiar with them. Then we may like them a lot!

On the next page, you'll have a chance to think about your culture. If you can, compare the way you filled out your sheet with the way other kids filled out theirs. How are you alike? How are you different? And could you have some fun if you got to know the "differences"?

Me and My Culture

My cultural background is_____

_____

_____.

I speak _____, and I'd like to

learn how to speak _____,

because_____.

My religious background is _____

_____.

In my family, we celebrate_____

and _____.

On my favorite holiday,_____,

we _____

_____

_____.

One of our special foods is _____

and it's_____!

Here's what I like about my culture: _____

_____

_____.

In short, I'd say I'm a _____

_____-American!

6 Who Are You Like?

Who's Like You?

You know, you belong to a *lot* of different groups. Let's look at some of them—

- You're a member of the human race.

- You're a female or you're a male.

- You're a kid.

- You belong to a racial, cultural, and probably a religious group (maybe more than one of each).

- You're a member of a neighbor-hood, a city, and a country.

- You're a member of a grade and of a school.

- You might belong to a group like the scouts or some other club.

- You're a member of a family.

Here's something new to think about. You're also part of a lot of groups that you **don't** know anything about. All over your town, all over this country, and all over the world, there are people with whom you share things, even though none of you may know it, and even though you don't know each other. In fact, you may all look so unlike each other that you'd never guess you **were** a group. It's kind of mysterious and curious to think that you have this hidden connection with people far away, or much older than you, or very different from you in a lot of ways.

Can you imagine what some of these groups might be?

Who else in your town has the same hobby you do? Who likes the same sport?

In this country, how many families are like yours?

How many people do you suppose there are all over the world who speak your language, belong to your religion, or celebrate the holidays you do?

Take a look at some of these statements. If one is true of you, stop and try to imagine who else it might be true of. Might they be far away from here? Might they be very old people? Might they be people who speak a different language or dress differently from you? Might they be of a different race than yours?

I like video games.
I can curl my tongue.
I hate trying to do something I'm not good at.
I love to draw pictures.
I'd like to be taller than I am.
I'm kind of scared of the dark.
I play softball.
I love cats.
I like to read.
I'd like to do something no one has ever done before.

Now look at these pictures and sentences. These are all pictures of and statements by people who live in the United States. Each of these statements has been made by one of these groups—A, B, C, or D.

Can you guess which statement belongs to which group?

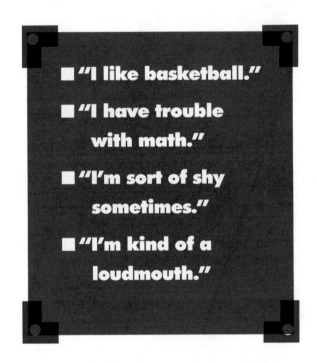

- "I like basketball."
- "I have trouble with math."
- "I'm sort of shy sometimes."
- "I'm kind of a loudmouth."

Are any of the statements above true of you, too? Are you surprised to see **WHO'S LIKE YOU?**

ANSWERS

Group A said, "I have trouble with math."
Group B said, "I'm sort of shy sometimes."
Group C said, "I like basketball."
Group D said, "I'm kind of a loudmouth."

Group A

Group B

Group C

Group D

You've come to the end of this book, and if you've been all the way through it, you've made a real portrait of yourself. You have a record of just who you are right now, right here.

Don't lose it! Put it in a safe place, and you'll enjoy looking at it later on in your life—next year, or when you're in high school, or even when you're grown up.

You can see from doing all these sheets that you're a person with many interests, skills, ideas, and feelings. You've thought about just where you are in the world. You've probably learned a lot about your family and its history. You've realized that you're part of a cultural group (or several) with whom you share important things—your language, your way of living, your holidays. And you've probably discovered that you have something in common with people who are in many other ways quite different from you.

You should feel pretty proud of yourself—for what you are, and for what you're learning.

And now, when you get to know other people, maybe you'll understand **them** a little better. You probably understand that everyone has favorite things, everyone has a family history, everyone has a culture. These may be a lot like yours, or they may be different. You could think about this when you meet new kids. What do **they** like to do? Do **they** have foods you'd like to try? Do **they** have games or celebrations you could enjoy? Give it a try!